Phoebe Koehler
The Day We Met You

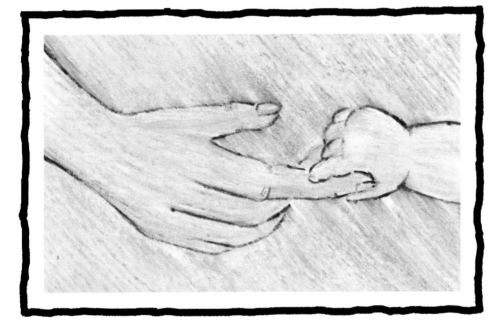

Afterword by Lois Ruskai Melina,
author of *Raising Adopted Children*

Aladdin Paperbacks

First Aladdin Paperbacks edition, May 1997
Copyright © 1990 by Phoebe Koehler

Aladdin Paperbacks
An imprint of Simon & Schuster
Children's Publishing Division
1230 Avenue of the Americas
New York, NY 10020

Also available in a Simon & Schuster Books for Young Readers edition.
Designed by Julie Quan
The text of this book was set in 28 point Galliard.
The illustrations were done in pastel crayon.
Printed in Hong Kong

10 9 8 7 6

The Library of Congress has cataloged the hardcover edition as follows:
Koehler, Phoebe.
The day we met you / by Phoebe Koehler. — 1st ed.
p.   cm.
Summary: Mom and Dad recount the exciting day when they adopted their baby.
ISBN 0-02-750901-X
[1. Adoption—Fiction.   2. Babies—Fiction.]   I. Title.
PZ7.K817725Day   1990
[E]—dc20   89-35344   CIP   AC

ISBN 0-689-80964-6 (Aladdin pbk.)

For Seth
and his wonderful parents,
Sharron and Joe

*T*he sun shone
bright the day
we met you.

They had called to say
we would be your parents.
How we hurried
to get things
ready!

We borrowed a car seat
so you could ride home safe.

We bought bottles
and formula
so you wouldn't
be hungry.

We bought diapers

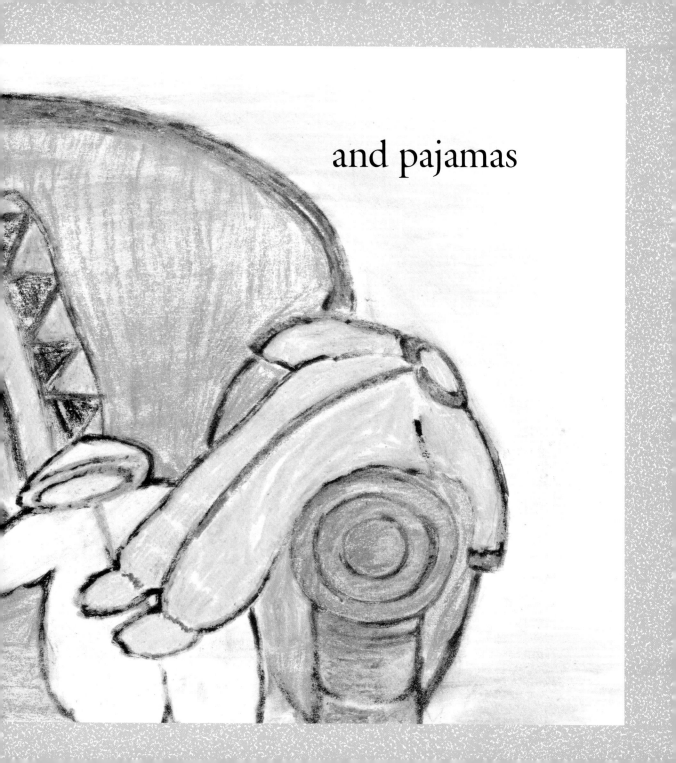

and pajamas

and shirts
and little socks

so you would be
dry and warm.

We found
some pacifiers
that looked
like butterflies

and a
mobile
full of
elephants.

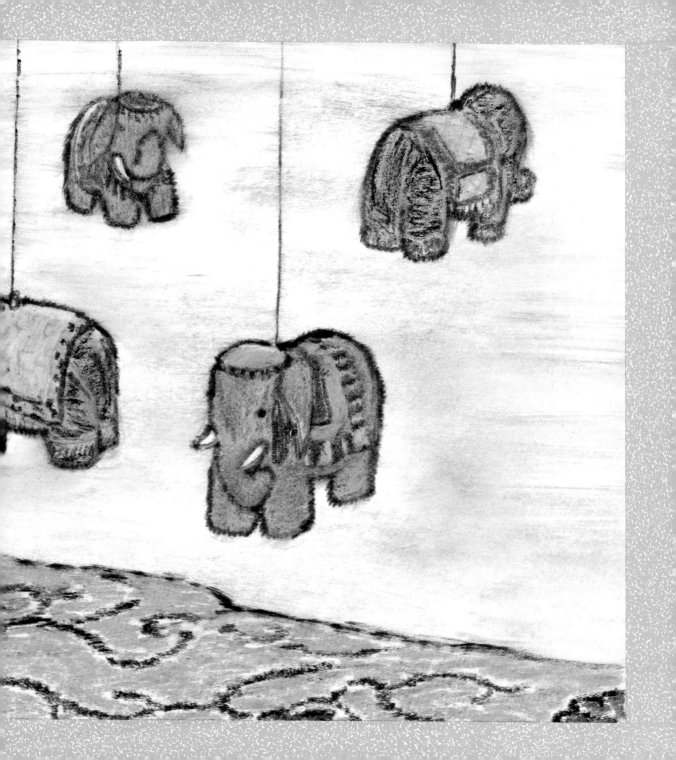

Grandpa
brought a
teddy bear
to keep you
company.

A friend
gave us a quilt
to cuddle you in.

A neighbor
lent us a cradle
so you could
sleep right next
to us.

We hung
wind chimes
in the window

and filled the room
with flowers.

Then we went
to get you. We
were very excited.

The minute
we saw you
we knew that
we loved you.

You felt
like the
sun
shining
inside us.

AFTERWORD

Perhaps no question is of more concern to adoptive parents than how and when they will tell their children they are adopted.

Phoebe Koehler's book demonstrates the best time to start is when parents are feeling warm and loving about their child.

She has told a simple story that parents can easily personalize as they read it aloud. Of course, it will be years before a child comprehends the full meaning of adoption. But talking about it with a young child lets her know that this is a topic the parents are comfortable with. Details to the story can be added as the child's ability to understand adoption grows.

It's important for parents to describe what happened in the child's life before they became a family—that the baby grew inside his birth mother *just like all babies do* and that he was born *just like all babies are born*. Because his birth mother couldn't take care of *any baby* born to her at that time, she made an adoption plan.

Parents may also want to talk about how the baby might have felt on her first night with her new parents. Perhaps the cradle seemed strange to a baby used to sleeping on a mat on the floor, as would be likely in some intercountry adoptions; or perhaps the formula tasted different than the milk she was used to.

While adoption is an experience in which we feel "the sun shining inside us," there are also elements of sadness in adoption. Parents who can acknowledge this right from the beginning give their children a marvelous gift—permission to express their feelings in a safe and comforting environment.

Lois Ruskai Melina is the author of *Making Sense of Adoption* and *Raising Adopted Children,* and is the editor and publisher of *Adopted Child* newsletter. She and her husband live in Moscow, Idaho, with their two children, who are both adopted.